Epitaph

by George Cameron Grant

CHARACTERS

Winston
Miguel, the Guide
C
Teenage Winston
Louise
Young Winston
The Old Man
Tommy
Man

My deepest appreciation goes out to the following: your generosity of time, talent, insight, and indefatigable encouragement is always a source of inspiration...

Richard Abramowitz

Liz Amadio

Father Douglas Arcoleo

Jeff Baltimore/XL Graphics, NYC

Vincent Bandille

John Borras

Tony Cucchiari

Phil Cutrone

Debra Decaro

Jon Freda

Olivia Horton

Robert Kamlot

Andrew Langton

Monsignor Jim Lisante

Mary Orzano

Sarah-Ann Rodgers

Michael Shapiro

Gene Silvers

Margo Singaliese

Heidi Voight

Susan Wasoff

Vicki Weidman

Larry Winer

...and especially to my daughters

Elizabeth & Jenna

*(**SCENE:** A cemetery. Headstone rests centerstage, front facing upstage.)*

*(**TIME:** A chilly October afternoon.)*

*(**AT RISE:** A cemetery **GUIDE**, dressed in a perfectly pressed black suit, dutifully enters upstage left, closely followed by a shivering, ruddy-faced **WINSTON**, hands stuffed into the pockets of a zippered wind breaker covering the sweater and jeans he wears…)*

GUIDE. I believe we'll find your parents right over…let's see…Galvin, Ward, Schmidt, Lohmann, should be…ah, here we are…McDonagh…Isabelle and – mmm, that's strange, doesn't seem to be any Francis marked on…

WINSTON. …there wouldn't be.

GUIDE. Why not?

WINSTON. Never had anything put there. Why do you think I asked for your stone carver to meet me here?

GUIDE. I assumed you were referring to an epitaph, not the actual name.

WINSTON. What's the difference?

GUIDE. According to our records, your father was interred over fifteen years ago.

WINSTON. There some kind of grave carving statute of limitations?

GUIDE. Not at all, it's just, well, somewhat irregular.

WINSTON. That was our relationship alright, somewhat irregular.

GUIDE. I see.

WINSTON. No, you don't.

GUIDE. Forgive me, I didn't mean to pry.

WINSTON. Sure you did, but that's OK, I imagine this kind of thing doesn't happen every day.

GUIDE. Actually, no, it doesn't.

WINSTON. Let's just say words never came easy between me and the Old Man, pleasant *or* otherwise, and the ones that did were usually loud enough to shatter the nearest hi-ball glass.

GUIDE. You didn't get along?

WINSTON. Talk about your big time understatement, *and* the reason I had no clue what to put on that damn stone in the first place.

GUIDE. *Aside* from his name, you mean.

WINSTON. Not that it's anybody's business, but I figured leaving his name off might motivate me to come up with the rest that much faster.

GUIDE. Does there have to be a rest?

WINSTON. *Everyone* should have a rest – a few words – something that sums up what their life was about – take my mom… *(reads from headstone)* "…Isabelle Anne McDonagh…Sister – Mother – Wife"…then, smack dab beneath the dates, complete with exclamation point and in quotes…"Sorrys Don't Count!"…see what I mean? A stranger could stop here and know exactly who she was in a heartbeat.

GUIDE. They'd know what she'd become, not necessarily who she was.

WINSTON. What's *that* supposed to mean?

GUIDE. It means that today is the day you finally get to put into stone who your *father* really was.

WINSTON. That's right…now where the hell's that carver?

GUIDE. Should be arriving any moment now.

WINSTON. I hope so… *(He shudders.)* …Aren't you cold?

GUIDE. Rather prefer it that way.

WINSTON. Guess it's better than boiling your tail off, but between you, me, and that crow licking his chops up there, I wouldn't exactly mind a glimpse of sunlight right about now – just a little too gothic out here for my taste.

GUIDE. May I be of any further assistance, Mr. McDonagh?

WINSTON. Winston.

GUIDE. Pardon me?

WINSTON. Name's Winston, Mr. McDonagh's the guy in the ground.

GUIDE. After Churchill?

WINSTON. No, Smith.

GUIDE. Smith?

WINSTON. Winston Smith. *1984?* The book? George Orwell?

GUIDE. Ah, yes, Mr. Orwell.

WINSTON. Always thought that was my father's twisted way of keeping me in line – *Big Brother watching* and all that jazz.

GUIDE. Being watched over isn't necessarily a bad thing.

WINSTON. Never did *me* any good, besides, he was too busy to watch.

GUIDE. Busy?

WINSTON. That's right. My Old Man had three passions – my mother, baseball, and reading…he used the walk-in closet of our apartment as an office – called it his Fortress of Solitude.

GUIDE. Fortress of…

WINSTON. …where Superman went to get away from it all?

GUIDE. Superman?

WINSTON. Skip it…anyway, it was really more like a bunker, filled to the ceiling with every kind of book, magazine or comic imaginable. You'd have to scream over mountains of crap and the noise of the black and white Zenith TV buried in there with him to get his attention, which really drove Mom up the wall, *especially* at dinner time. We'd joke that if the big one hit, all that would be left of the world would be him, the mountains of crap, that TV with the tin foil wrapped

WINSION. *(cont.)* around its busted antennae, and the roaches. He sure did love his books, they kept him sane – well, sort of sane – *safe* might be more like it.

GUIDE. Safe from what?

WINSTON. From what was on the other side, of course.

GUIDE. Well, if there isn't anything else…

WINSTON. …no, I'm fine, um, didn't catch the name.

GUIDE. Miguel.

WINSTON. Well, thanks for your help, Miguel.

MIGUEL. That's why I'm here. By the way, you might want to wander over to our grotto area, it's just beyond the cluster of holly right over there.

> *(…***WINSTON*** follows ***MIGUEL****'s pointed direction down-stage right…)*

WINSTON. Appreciate the tip… *(studying the grotto)* …mmm, weird.

MIGUEL. Pardon?

WINSTON. Nothing. Look, if you see that stone carver on the way back, do me a favor and tell him to hurry the hell…

> *(…***WINSTON*** scratches his head as he stares at the grotto…)*

MIGUEL. …there's something I think you should know about *him…*

> *(…A ***WOMAN****, appearing to be in her early 30s, enters behind them upstage left. White bandana around her head, she wears a ratty, puffy vest, feathery white down of which generously pokes through. It covers a denim shirt, utility belt lined with mallet and various chisels wrapped around the waist of her jeans, which are cuffed half way up mud-crusted construction boots…)*

WINSTON. …*very* weird.

WOMAN. What's that?

> *(…They turn toward the ***WOMAN****…)*

MIGUEL. Ah! You've arrived.

WOMAN. Hope I haven't kept anyone waiting.

WINSTON. Who are *you?*

MIGUEL. That's him…I mean, her.

WINSTON. Who?

WOMAN. Your mason, of course, I'm here to carve…

WINSTON. …*you're* the carver?

WOMAN. And you were expecting?

WINSTON. Not *you.*

MIGUEL. If you'll excuse me, there's a line back at the gate.

WOMAN. Thank you, Miguel.

MIGUEL. I trust I've been helpful.

WINSTON. Oh, yeah…sure…thanks.

MIGUEL. You're perfectly welcome. Have a peaceful visit, Winston.

(…**MIGUEL** *withdraws into the shadows…*)

WINSTON. Of course I'll have a peaceful visit, why *wouldn't* I have…

(…*He turns toward* **MIGUEL**, *who's already gone…*)

WOMAN. …Winston?

WINSTON. That's right, as in…

WOMAN. …Orwell, I know.

WINSTON. You do?

WOMAN. Sure…big fan.

WINSTON. Big fan or big ears?

WOMAN. Don't worry, Big Brother, or in my case, Big *Sister,* isn't watching *or* listening, I just love his work, that's all.

WINSTON. Yeah, sure.

WOMAN. Ever read *Animal Farm?*

WINSTON. In high school, like everyone else, that doesn't prove…

WOMAN. …what about *Down And Out In Paris And London?*

WINSTON. What the hell is…

WOMAN. …His real name wasn't George, you know, it was Eric…

WINSTON. …alright, I believe you, whoever you are – who *are* you?

WOMAN. I told you, I'm the stone carver.

WINSTON. I know *what* you are, but *who* are you? What's your name?

WOMAN. They call me C.

WINSTON. Just C?

C. It's short for…carver.

WINSTON. *Very* short.

C. To the point.

> (…*Holds up her chisel…*)

WINSTON. Very funny.

> (…*Looking around, he begins swatting something away from his face…*)

WINSTON. What's with all the feathers?

C. Afraid that's me… *(grabbing her vest)* …I've had this thing forever…tend to leave a trail wherever I go.

WINSTON. Thanks, should make it a lot easier finding my way out.

C. Glad I could be of help…so what was weird?

WINSTON. Huh?

C. When I walked in on you and Miguel…

WINSTON. …no big deal, he was pointing out the grotto over there.

C. Beautiful, isn't it?

WINSTON. Very, and I was just about to say how weird it was that…are you sure you're here to carve my father's headstone?

C. Why, something wrong with that?

WINSTON. No, not at all, it's just…how long have you done this?

C. Look, Winston, I know what I'm doing. Your father's in very capable hands, don't worry.

WINSTON. You just seem so…

C. …young? Female?

WINSTON. Yes, and yes.

C. Take a closer look at that grotto…

> (…*They look out toward the grotto…*)

C. …see all those statues surrounding it?

WINSTON. Hard to miss, they're everywhere.

C. Well, they're all mine.

WINSTON. You own them?

C. I *carved* them.

WINSTON. What?

C. That's right.

WINSTON. I don't believe…

C. …each and every one of them.

WINSTON. Wow, I'm impressed.

C. Does that mean I pass the audition?

WINSTON. Cute.

C. So I've been told.

WINSTON. If you're really *that* good, how come you're doing *this*?

C. A girl can't win with you, Winston, a minute ago I wasn't good enough, now I'm *too* good.

WINSTON. That's truer than you can imagine.

C. Don't be so sure…shall we begin?

WINSTON. You're the boss.

> (…*She kneels, unfastens her tool belt, and rests it before the headstone…*)

C. Let's see, so far we have Francis Xavier McDonagh, Born August 21, 1911, Died…

WINSTON. …how do you know all that?

C. Didn't they tell you?

WINSTON. Tell me what?

C. I'm known as C, the psychic mason.

> *(…He stares at her for an unsure, exaggerated moment…)*

WINSTON. Bull crap.

> *(…She laughs…)*

C. Almost had you there…office gave me the details.

WINSTON. You're a funny lady, you know that?

C. I'd do my whole routine, but, as Miguel said, there's a line.

WINSTON. For lousy comedy?

C. For this…*(holds up her chisel)* …you'd be surprised how many loose ends there are out there, how much unfinished business there is…would you like me to leave room for something after the name and dates?

WINSTON. Sure.

C. And what would that something be?

WINSTON. I'm working on it.

> *(…She stares at him…)*

WINSTON. I know, I know, it's been a while.

C. I *do* have to get back *eventually*.

WINSTON. That makes two of us.

C. I'll start while you think.

> *(…Picking up the mallet, she begins carving into the stone…)*

C. So are you going to tell me what's so weird about my grotto?

WINSTON. When I was a little kid, my Old Man used to take me to a place in the neighborhood just like that.

C. Really?

WINSTON. St. Lucy's. Sort of looked like the Alamo – you know, that old Mexican mission where…

C. …I remember.

WINSTON. What?

C. Remember? The Alamo?

WINSTON. *As I was saying…*Davy Crockett was always a hero of mine, and the fact that he died at the Alamo – well, *that's* probably the reason I liked going to St. Lucy's in the first place.

C. Boys will be boys.

WINSTON. Every Saturday it was baseball practice, lunch at White Castle, then the Alamo. Hell, for a kid that's damn near perfect – like being Babe Ruth, Prince Valiant, and Davy Crockett all in one day.

(*…She points her chisel downstage right…*)

C. The Babe's right down the road there.

WINSTON. Get outta' here!

C. Serious.

WINSTON. Really?

C. Just on the other side of my weird grotto.

WINSTON. The Old Man would have liked that.

C. How do you know he didn't know?

WINSTON. I don't.

C. Would you like me to spell out the Xavier or just go with the initial?

WINSTON. Just the initial, he hated it spelled out, thought the X sounded more official – less saint-like.

C. Heaven forbid.

WINSTON. Hey, don't get me wrong, I've got nothing against it, but the Old Man, that's another story.

C. Really.

WINSTON. Let's just say the subject of religion was pretty much off the table. Don't remember *ever* being inside a church with him – St. Lucy's or any *other* for that matter.

C. Didn't your family ever go to Mass?

WINSTON. Sure. Well, sort of. Sundays I'd go to the eight o'clock kids mass, so Mom and the Old Man would just be leaving the apartment as I'd be getting back. She preferred the nine, which we called *the long one* – solid hour unless Monsignor Brady was giving the homily, in which case all bets were off.

C. Then they *did* go.

WINSTON. They *left* together, so I always assumed they went *in* together, but at her funeral several years later, Louise Regan, the building busy body, ratted him out…

> (…*lights down on* **WINSTON** *and* **C,** *up downstage right on* **LOUISE,** *a woman of 60 dressed in formal mourning, gripping the handbag in her lap with one hand, weeping into the handkerchief she clutches in the other… she sits next to a dour* **TEENAGE WINSTON,** *wrinkled white shirt perfectly matching his too-small confirmation suit…both* **WINSTON** *and* **LOUISE** *sit on folding chairs…*)

LOUISE. I was sorry to hear about your mother, Winston.

TEENAGE WINSTON. Thank you, Mrs. Regan.

LOUISE. She was a very devout woman, your mother was.

TEENAGE WINSTON. Yes, I know.

LOUISE. Never missed a Sunday that I can remember, and since *I've* never missed one – except, of course, for that Sunday morning I was having Harold, my youngest – but that's the Lord's work also, isn't it?

TEENAGE WINSTON. Uh, yeah…I guess so.

LOUISE. Your father, though, well, that's another story.

TEENAGE WINSTON. What's *that* supposed to mean?

LOUISE. Strange, him not being a church going fellow and all, married to such a religious woman.

TEENAGE WINSTON. What are you talking about?

LOUISE. I'm talking about your father never going to mass.

TEENAGE WINSTON. He went to the nine with my mother every Sunday.

LOUISE. He went, alright, but he never went *in*. Every Sunday the ladies and I would watch and wave as they'd drive up to the church. She'd step out of the car, come over to greet us, then we'd all climb the stairs and walk in together – all of us, that is, except your father. He'd just sit there in the car with the motor running, and that's where we'd find him *after* mass, waiting for your mother. She'd wish us a blessed Sunday, walk to the idling car, climb in, and off he'd drive. I tell you, I just don't know how she put up with it.

TEENAGE WINSTON. That's a lie.

LOUISE. Excuse me?

TEENAGE WINSTON. All of it, all lies, you're a liar, *a no good rotten liar.*

LOUISE. Well, aren't *you* the poison apple that fell from the rotting tree.

TEENAGE WINSTON. Why don't you just take your stupid lies and leave me alone.

LOUISE. I have a good mind to walk right over to your father and let him know exactly what a freshmouth he has for a son.

TEENAGE WINSTON. In that case, I'll give you something to *really* complain about – *kiss my freakin' ass cheeks, lady!*

(*…***LOUISE** *gasps and recoils…*)

LOUISE. Monster… *(She retreats several steps.)* …Monster!

(*…He bares imaginary fangs and growls – she exits – lights go dark on* **TEENAGE WINSTON**, *back up on* **WINSTON** *and* **C**…)

WINSTON. She told my Old Man alright, and he told *her* that she could kiss *his* ass in Macy's window right after she got through kissing *mine.*

C. He backed you up.

WINSTON. Yeah…guess he did.

C. Why not? You stood up for *him.*

WINSTON. Of course, I…that's right, I did.

C. So where do you think he went?

WINSTON. What do you mean?

C. While your mom was in church, where do you think he went?

WINSTON. Who said he went anywhere?

C. How do you know he didn't?

WINSTON. Why would you think he did?

C. I don't know.

WINSTON. Always figured he just stayed there and waited for her.

C. You're probably right.

WINSTON. Don't patronize me.

C. I'm not, I'm sure you're perfectly right.

WINSTON. Wanna' know perfect?

C. Have *my* idea of perfect, what's *yours?*

WINSTON. Hearing them climb the stairs after mass, knowing the Old Man held a stuffed white bakery bag, which I'd grab and open before they even made it through the front door, inhaling as deeply as I could before removing the one jelly donut that had been waiting for me in that donut rack all morning long.

C. Sweet.

WINSTON. I'd turn that baby on its side, and suck out every last drop of jelly – now *that's* perfect.

C. Believe it or not, I understand.

WINSTON. Yeah, right.

C. Really, I do.

WINSTON. So what's perfect to *you?*

C. *Making* the donut.

WINSTON. What?

C. Or in my case, the sculpture, *but not just making it,* making it so well that people feel about it exactly the way you feel about that donut.

WINSTON. Well, for what's it's worth… *(looks over at the grotto)* … I think you'd make a damn fine donut.

C. That's worth a lot, Winston, thank you.

WINSTON. Just tellin' it like I see it.

C. Then tell me this. If your father hated church, and couldn't stand religion, why would he take you to St. Lucy's when he could have taken you anywhere?

WINSTON. Because of the grotto.

C. Not one as weird as mine, I hope.

WINSTON. Weirder! Taking up the entire corner, right next to St. Lucy's, was this big ass grotto with sculptures of Jesus, Mary, Joseph, all the usual suspects, everywhere you looked, looking down on you, *watching* over you, over *everyone,* and right there at the center of it all was a waterfall, a waterfall exactly like that one over there.

C. Sounds like I'd feel right at home.

WINSTON. There sure were a lot who did. They came from all over just to touch the statues – kneel, pray, light their candles, fill their empty mayonnaise jars, soda cups, holy water bottles, whatever they had – place was knee deep in crutches, canes, walkers, rusty abandoned wheelchairs – they called it the Bronx Lourdes, if you can believe *that.*

C. Don't you think people need a place like that?

WINSTON. Why, to break their hearts? It's a fantasy, C, *all of it.*

C. So of all the places this non-believing father of yours could have taken you on a weekly basis, he takes you to holy ground, a place of miracles?

WINSTON. Had nothing to do with miracles, he took me there because I liked it.

C. Or did you like it because he took you there?

WINSTON. Stop twisting my words.

C. Maybe he took you there because *he* wanted to be there.

WINSTON. And why the hell would *he* want to be there?

C. *Everybody* wants a miracle, Winston, even those who don't believe in them, and *especially* those who do and don't want to admit they do.

WINSTON. And what do you think happened to all those grotto people once they finished their precious pilgrimage? I mean, long after the grotto candles burned out, long after the grotto water was showered out of their hair, off their aching bodies, or pissed out of their systems? Long after they went back home to the same old roach and rat infested dumps they were praying their grotto god would get them out of, what do you think *really* happened?

C. *You* tell *me.*

WINSTON. The worst thing possible.

C. What's that?

WINSTON. Nothing.

C. Nothing?

WINSTON. Nothing. No limbs healed. No cancers cured. No broken hearts salvaged. No dreams come true. No souls saved. No prayers answered. *Nothing.*

C. Then how do you explain the crutches, walkers, wheelchairs…

WINSTON. …the power of suggestion *and* the used medical supply store three blocks away, which probably sold them their own stuff back before the week was over – some miracle.

C. Why would you even *think* something like that?

WINSTON. Because no one – and I mean *no one* – *ever* prayed harder than I did, and *my* prayers were *never* answered. That's right, you heard me – there's my dirty little secret – I was one of *them.* Just call me *Grotto Boy.* I'll have you know you're looking at a former believer, a one hundred per cent, dyed in the wool, totally in the tank for the big guy true believer. I was even an altar boy – damn fine one at that – trudging through the wind-swept snow at five every morning, plastic-shrouded cassock and alb dutifully slung over my shoulder – for a moment there they even had me thinking priest – a *very* brief moment. Oh yeah, I knelt,

I prayed, I drank, I partook, I mopped up, I believed. Sometimes during those weekly grotto visits, while the Old Man was cat napping on the bench, I'd sneak into St. Lucy's, bless myself, then make my pitch to that painted plaster of paris guy hanging on the wooden cross…

(…*lights down on* **WINSTON** *and* **C,** *up on a park bench downstage right and a pew downstage left…* **WINSTON'S FATHER,** *seen from behind, is bent over and nodding on the bench facing upstage, as the silhouette of a crucifix shadows the pew facing downstage…dressed in a little league outfit,* **YOUNG WINSTON,** *who's been staring at his* **SLEEPING FATHER,** *runs cross-stage to the pew, where he kneels, a light from below illuminating his face…*)

YOUNG WINSTON. Jesus, it's me, it's Winston, you know, *Winston,* the kid you're always watchin', always checkin' up on. Look, Jesus, it's like this, you know what's been goin' on at home, you know how good I've been, how hard I've tried to hang in there just like you did, but I sure could use some help with Mom, she keeps gettin' worse and worse. I keep pourin' it down the drain, the Old Man keeps bringin' it in, then he dives into the bunker to hide, leavin' me holdin' the bag of empties, so whatta' ya' say, huh? Ease up on the curve balls and throw me a nice fat one right down the middle for a change. Hello? If you're there, and you can hear me, I could use a little help, OK? Please? Hello? *Hello? HELLO?*

(…*Lights down on bench and pew, back up on* **WINSTON** *and* **C.**…)

WINSTON. So after a few minutes of silence I'd get up, leave the church, shake the Old Man up, and then he'd cart me off to Mickey's Tavern, where he sat himself down on his favorite stool with me right next to him, and in no time I'd be dive-bombin' pretzels into an exploding coke, while he'd be depth-chargin' boilermakers

WINSTON. *(cont.)* into a belly full of detonated dreams. At some point he'd fall off the stool, and I'd catch him just before his drooling puss hit the saw dust – lucky for me the gin mill was in stumbling distance from our apartment. So much for Grotto Boy. So much for miracles. But I have to admit, the grotto *did* eventually serve a purpose.

C. Which was…

WINSTON. …burrowed into the base of the mountain that served as the perimeter of said grotto, was a cave – sort of a religious fanatic funhouse, Tunnel of Holy Love. You'd walk in at one end, and every ten feet there'd be another wacky religious scene carved into the rock, protected by a slab of delinquent-proof glass.

C. What kinds of scenes?

WINSTON. Bloody stuff mostly, barely lit by rows and rows of votive candles. I'm talkin' upside-down crucifix-ions, beheadings, whippings, eye-gougings, you know, all that crown of thorns martyrdom jazz – demented, spooky and exciting all at the same time, and all of them protected by the glass, but what was protecting *us* from *them*, that's what I'd like to know? I mean, how could you *not* walk out of there all messed up? But as we got older, it also became a hell of a place to take your best girl – you know, somewhere dry, warm and scary to hide out, hang out, and, when she got freaked out, *make* out.

C. With no one watching.

WINSTON. Exactly.

C. You weren't afraid of getting caught?

WINSTON. That was part of the thrill.

C. Some might have considered such a thing, I don't know, sacrilegious maybe?

WINSTON. While others might have considered exposing kids to the crazy stuff behind that glass a lot more sac-rilegious than any of the *crazier* stuff happening *this* side of it, but in the end it didn't really matter, we were all a bunch of jerks for even being there in first place.

C. Why, for wanting to believe in something?

WINSTON. No, for believing in something that always left us wanting.

C. And what do *you* want, Winston?

WINSTON. Right now? I just want to get this done and get on with whatever I have to get on with…you almost finished?

C. *You* tell *me*.

WINSTON. What do we have so far?

C. Francis X. McDonagh. Born August 21, 1911. Died…

WINSTON. …I know when he died, what else?

C. That's it…so far.

WINSTON. Crap.

> (…*swatting more feathers away,* WINSTON *walks down-stage right, pacing before the stone, which he suddenly pounding…*)

WINSTON. *(under his breath)* Bastard… *(screams)* …*you miserable, selfish bastard!*

C. Like that with an exclamation point, in quotes, or both?

WINSTON. What?

C. The *miserable, selfish bastard,* would you like it…

WINSTON. …oh, you just keep getting funnier, don't you?

C. I'm not trying to be funny, Winston, just trying to pay attention to someone who's clearly in a lot of pain.

WINSTON. Lucky me, I ask for a stone carver, I get a comedian *and* grief counselor thrown in for the same, low, low price. Well, take my advice, Lady, stick to what you do best.

C. Can't tell you how many times I've seen a single moment of truth heal a lifetime of pain.

WINSTON. Lifetime of…who the hell do you think you are?

C. Just a stone carver.

WINSTON. Then shut up and carve!

C. I'm waiting.

WINSTON. For what?

C. For something to carve.

WINSTON. I've got something for you to carve...*go to hell!*

> (...*Lowering her head, then her tools, she begins sliding them back into the belt...*)

C. Perhaps you really *are* done after all.

> (...*Wrapping the belt around her waist, she stands...*)

WINSTON. I'm sorry, OK?

C. Goodbye, Winston.

> (...*She turns and begins walking away...*)

WINSTON. Wait...*C!*

> (...*She keeps walking...*)

WINSTON. Come on, don't do this.

> (...*She is halfway in the shadows...*)

WINSTON. *He wasn't cat napping, alright?*

> (...*She stops and looks back...*)

C. Excuse me?

WINSTON. My Old Man. He wasn't cat napping.

C. What *was* he doing?

WINSTON. He was...crying.

C. Crying?

> (...*Lights stay up on **WINSTON** and C as they turn to look downstage...Lights come back up on the bench, pew, and **YOUNG WINSTON**, who stares at his trembling and weeping **FATHER**, again seen from behind on the bench...*)

YOUNG WINSTON. Dad...hey Dad...*DAD!* Come on, Dad, you gotta' cut that out.

> (...**YOUNG WINSTON** *pulls at his **FATHER**'s sleeve, but he yanks it away, as the watching, now tearful, **WINSTON**, still upstage, goes to his knees...*)

YOUNG WINSTON. Everybody's starin' at us...some of the girls in my class are at the grotto and they're lookin' right over here…why are you always doin' this? What's *wrong* with you?

WINSTON. Would you just stop it.

YOUNG WINSTON. Can we get out of here already?

WINSTON. *Please!*

YOUNG WINSTON. Dad?

WINSTON & YOUNG WINSTON. *Dad!*

> (*…a self-conscious* **YOUNG WINSTON** *looks around, backs up, then bolts toward the pew, where he kneels, folds his hands, and looks up – lights down on him and the bench as* **WINSTON** *wipes his eyes…*)

WINSTON. Happy now?

> (*…***C** *removes the bandana from her head, unfurls, then dangles it over his shoulder…*)

C. Here.

> (*…***WINSTON** *turns away…*)

C. Go ahead, take it – don't worry, it's clean.

> (*…He takes the bandana, sniffs it, then wipes his eyes and face…*)

WINSTON. Gettin' hot out here all of a sudden.

C. Must have been very hard for you.

WINSTON. Hard for *me? That's* funny. Week after week, my Old Man sits on that bench, crying his eyes out in front of everyone, and do I ever ask him why? Do I ever try to comfort him? Make him feel like somebody gives a crap? That *I* give a crap? No, I just run, I desert him and run. Now *you* tell *me* who the miserable, selfish bastard is.

C. You were just a kid, Winston.

WINSTON. So was *he* once, think anyone gave a crap about him then either?

C. I don't know, do you?

> (*…Stuffing the bandana into his coat pocket, he stands, removes a wallet from his back pocket, then a business card from it, which he extends to* **C***…*)

WINSTON. Here.

C. What's this?

WINSTON. Take it…go ahead.

> (…*She does, reading it…*)

C. Francis X. McDonagh – Consultant.

WINSTON. When I went through the apartment, you know, after he died, I found boxes and boxes of those buried underneath his Fortress of Solitude mountains.

C. Says he was a consultant. What did he consult?

WINSTON. Anything. Everything. Know those kinds of people who know a little about a lot of things?

C. I've met a few.

WINSTON. Well, he knew a *lot* about a *lot* of things. Sure, some of that came from all the reading he did, but most of it came from just being so damn smart…would you believe he was six months away from graduating head of his class at Fordham?

C. How *did* he finish?

WINSTON. He didn't.

C. Why not?

WINSTON. Christmas Eve, senior year, *his* Old Man came home the morning after his holiday office party to announce he'd lost every penny they had in an over-night poker game.

C. Didn't your family have had anything put away for…

WINSTON. …*when I said every penny, I meant every penny.* In a blink of an eye, he went from big man on campus to bread winner for a suicidal father, rageful mother, and terrified baby brother. Merry Christmas, Frankie, now get your ass out there and find a job.

C. That stinks.

WINSTON. Stinks? That's a game changer, C, a soul crusher, that's *screw your dreams, the rent is due.*

C. How did he earn a living?

WINSTON. He didn't earn a living, he existed, just like everyone else. It was the Depression, you didn't get fat, you got
by – *if* you were lucky. Here was someone who just
knew how things worked, what made things tick, could
pull an engine apart and put it back together without
a manual, but put his life back together? Not a chance.
He could never make *anything* happen, and it seemed
like every time he *did* come close to whatever star he
reached for, something would bubble up from the
sewer, grab him by the ankle, and pull him right back
down to earth. Sure, there was the occasional proj-
ect, pipe dream here, hair-brained scheme there, but
most of his time was spent driving a taxi up, down, and
across this freakin' city. Hey, don't get me wrong, in
those days hackin' was a great way to earn an honest
living, but this was a man who truly had greatness written into his genetic code – his family knew it, *he* knew
it, and when he met my mother at 17, *she* knew it, but
by the time *I* finally came around, he'd already fallen
from *I'm somebody* to *I'm sorry*, and, as she constantly
reminded him then, and anyone who walks by this
grave now, *sorrys don't count.*

(…He begins laughing…)

C. What's so funny?

(…and again takes out his wallet…)

WINSTON. He always warned me never to let my chauffeur's
license expire, just in case I got into a jam and needed
a way to make a few extra bucks… *(proudly extending the
open wallet)* …Still got it.

C. Have you ever needed it?

WINSTON. Are you kidding? I'm a writer, writers *always*
need a way to make some extra money, especially
writers with two kids. I've done my share of hackin',
believe me.

C. So I guess that was sound advice?

WINSTON. Hate admitting it, but his advice usually was, and he'd give it to anybody who'd listen, even those who didn't want it or couldn't care less. Anyone who climbed into his cab got some kind of opinion, with one of those cards slapped into their palm as a reminder of where it came from.

C. Here.

(*…She extends the business card…*)

WINSTON. Keep it, I've got boxes of them.

C. Think I will…thanks.

(*…She tucks it into her vest…*)

WINSTON. He honestly believed one day he'd hand one of those things to a stranger, and they'd hand him back a second chance, instead of just a handful of loose change.

C. So he *did* believe in miracles.

WINSTON. Right up until that morning they found him slumped over the wheel of his cab, in front of the grotto, motor still running.

C. How did he…

WINSTON. …death certificate said coronary, but I know what really killed him.

C. What was that?

WINSTON. What I didn't find out until the day of his funeral – walked into Carrera Brothers funeral parlor, and sitting right in the middle of the front row was his baby brother Tommy.

(*…lights down on* **WINSTON** *and* **C**, *up stage right on a black-suited* **TOMMY McDONAGH**, *a large man in his late-50s, sitting at the middle of three metal folding chairs, bowed head cupped in his meaty hands, sobbing, as* **WINSTON** *approaches him…*)

WINSTON. Hey, Unc.

(*…Startled,* **TOMMY** *looks up at* **WINSTON**, *then struggles to his feet…*)

TOMMY. Hey there, kid.

(*…Wiping away tears, he swallows* **WINSTON** *in a bear hug…*)

TOMMY. Sorry about your dad.

WINSTON. Thanks, Unc.

TOMMY. He was a good man, kid, always tried to do the right thing.

WINSTON. I know.

(*…Wrapping his arm around* **WINSTON**'s *shoulder, he leads him to the chairs…*)

TOMMY. Come, sit, sit…aw, jeez, I mean *after* you say hello to Dad, of course.

(*…He begins leading him downstage, but* **WINSTON** *stops…*)

WINSTON. It's alright, I've been here since six am, he's gotta' be sick of me by now.

TOMMY. Not a chance, kid…

(*…They sit…*)

TOMMY. …your dad admired you, worshipped the ground you walked on.

WINSTON. Yeah, sure.

TOMMY. He did. Look, I know he and I hardly ever talked, but when we did, it was always about you – Winston did this, Winston did that, you should see how far Winston smacked the ball today – he always wanted you to be a big time ball player, like he always wanted to be.

WINSTON. Yeah, well life's got this nasty habit of changin' those well made plans, doesn't it?

TOMMY. Didn't have to tell *him* that. He loved you, kid.

WINSTON. Would have been nice if he told me that once in a while.

TOMMY. Trust me, he loved you *and* your girls – how are they, by the way?

WINSTON. Doing great, Unc, they're in high school now.

TOMMY. High school? You gotta' be kiddin' me.

WINSTON. They've been living with me for the past five years.

TOMMY. Sorry to hear about you and…

WINSTON. …don't be.

TOMMY. From what your Aunt Gerry tells me they're great girls, which doesn't surprise me.

WINSTON. No fatalities so far.

TOMMY. *(looking around)* Are they here?

WINSTON. No, I told them to go to school, they'll be here tonight. Thanks for coming, Unc.

TOMMY. Listen, Winston, I know you two had your problems and all, but just try to understand how hard things were for him. I pretty much had a free ride, but only because he was doin' the heavy liftin' for *all* of us.

WINSTON. That was the rumor.

TOMMY. Frankie had the world by the balls until it fell on him.

WINSTON. Yeah, I heard the gambling story.

TOMMY. Oh, he bounced back from that *and* everything else that came his way, but he never recovered from the Cubs thing.

WINSTON. Cubs thing? *What* Cubs thing?

TOMMY. You know, the accident, the training camp accident.

WINSTON. Sorry, Unc, but I don't know what the hell you're talking about.

*(…***TOMMY*** stares at* ***WINSTON****, incredulous…)*

TOMMY. He never told you, did he?

WINSTON. Told me what?

TOMMY. Winston, your Old Man was the greatest third baseman I ever saw play the game. He was only the star of the Fordham Rams, that's all, checked out by every club in the majors.

WINSTON. Get outta' here.

TOMMY. Honest injun' – near the end of his junior year he was approached by a Cubs scout…

WINSTON. …*Chicago* Cubs?

TOMMY. That's right – handed over a business card and offered him a Triple A contract right there on the spot.

WINSTON. You kiddin' me?

TOMMY. I kid you not, but Frankie walked a straight line, always played things right down the middle, so he told Mister Cubs to come back the following June, 'cause he was gettin' that diploma come hell or high water.

WINSTON. Jeez, what the hell was he thinking?

TOMMY. Nobody could figure *that* out, *especially* your mom, who'd already been dating him for three years, and figured she had a little leverage, but he wouldn't budge, not one inch, not for her, not for anyone. I mean, this was 1930, grown men out there beggin' for a day's pay, and there's your Old Man's turnin' down a contract to play pro ball, but that was Frankie, *stubborn* as a mule once he made his mind up about somethin'.

WINSTON. Don't believe what you're telling me here.

TOMMY. So he starts his senior year with life lookin' better than anyone had a right to in those days, when *whammo!* He gets sucked into our old man's nightmare, has to quit Fordham in the middle of his final year, and finds himself out on the street with all the other hard luck cases. Eventually he scrounges up some piece work at Pelham stables, shoveling mud and horse manure, when suddenly he drops the shovel, runs home, digs the business card out of his night stand, calls Mister Cubs and tells him, "Yessir, after careful consideration, I've decided to entertain whatever offer you had in mind."

WINSTON. No way!

TOMMY. Oh, yeah, so the scout comes back to New York, takes Frankie and our Old Man out for a steak dinner, and by the time dessert comes, your father's a member of the Cubs farm team. Within two weeks of spring training, he's proven himself to be the best investment they ever made, and they're talkin' Major Leagues by late May.

WINSTON. I'm confused here, Unc, if all of this actually happened…

TOMMY. …oh, it happened, alright.

WINSTON. Then why do I feel like I've lived a different life than the life I should have lived?

TOMMY. 'Cause just when your Old Man thought he'd taken on the world and kicked its ass, the world decided it would take another whack at him – only this time when he wasn't lookin'.

WINSTON. I don't get it.

TOMMY. One day he was suitin' up, gettin' ready to hit the field, when Mister Cubs walked up to his locker and told him to enjoy the game 'cause it was goin' to be his last – in the minors, that is – *they were shippin' him out to Wrigley that weekend!*

WINSTON. Get outta'…

TOMMY. …he was out of his mind, callin' us on the manager's phone, screamin' like a lunatic – we *all* were – and then he hit the field…

WINSTON. …yeah, and…

TOMMY. …he was havin' himself a good game – no, a *great* game – and there he was, in the on-deck circle takin' his cuts when…it happened.

WINSTON. What?

TOMMY. Their big slugger Moe Willis was at the plate. Down 0 and 2, he gets faked out by a wicked scroogie that spins him 'round full circle, but *not* before lettin' go of the bat, which pinwheels toward the on-deck circle and whacks your Old Man on the side of the head…

WINSTON. …holy…

TOMMY. …he goes down hard, and everyone in that park's thinkin' *dead man,* like it's gonna' take a miracle for him to get back up, but son-of-a-bitch, after about ten minutes, he does. Only the Frankie that gets up is *not* the Frankie that went down. They bring him into the clubhouse, take him to the hospital, give him the nose-to-hose, then break the bad news.

WINSTON. What bad news?

TOMMY. Right eye. Damaged by the shot to the head – permanently. Game over. Career over. Dream over.

WINSTON. I can't believe he never told me any of this.

TOMMY. Neither can I.

WINSTON. Why the hell would he keep this from me?

TOMMY. I don't know, maybe he was ashamed.

WINSTON. Ashamed? That he was a freakin' Chicago Cub?

TOMMY. Maybe he saw it as a failure, you know, comin' that close and not makin' it.

WINSTON. But it wasn't his fault! *None* of it was his fault.

TOMMY. Guess he didn't see it that way.

WINSTON. And I was always such a creep to him.

TOMMY. Don't beat yourself up, kid. Look, I loved your father, I really did, but he never made lovin' him easy, maybe now you have a better idea why.

WINSTON. He would have been my idol.

TOMMY. Who says he can't be your idol *now?* Tellin' ya', Winston, I wish you could've seen him play.

WINSTON. So do I.

TOMMY. He hadn't been there two weeks, the team already had a nickname for him – called him *Frankie the Vac.*

WINSTON. *Frankie the Vac?*

TOMMY. Yeah, 'cause anything that got hit to his side of the field he sucked right up… *(He belly-laughs.)* …yep, that's what they called him, alright, *Frankie the Vac.*

WINSTON. *Frankie the Vac, Frankie the…*

*(…***WINSTON*** *suddenly leaps from the chair as* ***TOMMY*** *falls into darkness, and lights come back up on* **C.***…)*

WINSTON. …that's it!

C. What's it?

WINSTON. *That's* what you put there, that's what you carve into that stone, smack dab in the middle of that empty space beneath his name, as large and as deep as you can carve it – exclamation point, quote marks, the works…*Frankie the Vac!*

C. It's perfect, Winston.

WINSTON. You think?

C. *Absolutely* perfect.

(…*Kneeling,* **C** *begins carving the Epitaph on the stone…*)

WINSTON. Yep, that's him, alright… *(proudly)* …sucked up *everything* that got hit to his side of the field.

C. Nice to have someone to look up to…someone to believe in.

(…**WINSTON** *looks up…*)

WINSTON. Hey, C, you think he might be, uh…I don't know…lookin' down, watchin' us right now?

C. Can't imagine why he *wouldn't* be.

WINSTON. I just want him to know that I finally got here, finally got to put into stone what had to be said.

C. I'm sure he does, and I'm sure he appreciates it.

(…*Bending down, he takes a closer look at what she's carving…*)

WINSTON. Jeez, you really *are* good.

C. Thank you, Winston.

WINSTON. That's deep enough, right?

C. More than enough.

WINSTON. Gotta' last forever.

C. Don't worry, Winston, it will.

(…**WINSTON** *slowly unzips his jacket, taking out a small plastic bag, the rustling of which gets* **C***'s attention…*)

C. What's that?

WINSTON. A little somethin' I picked up for him along the way.

C. What is it?

(…*Opening the bag, he removes a brand new Chicago Cubs baseball cap, tag still hanging from its side…*)

C. He'll love that, Winston.

WINSTON. You think so?

C. I *know* so… (*She stops chiseling.*) …there – finished. What do *you* think?

(…*He comes around, bends and takes a close look at the stone, running his fingers across the inscription…*)

WINSTON. You sure make a nice donut, lady.

C. And who'd know that better than you?

(…*They laugh…*)

WINSTON. Best third baseman he ever saw, that's what Tommy said.

(…*She steps aside as he drops to one knee before the stone…*)

WINSTON. Here you go, Dad, this belongs to you.

(…*Brushing the cap off, he gently lays it before the stone…C reaches out for him from behind, almost touching his shoulder as he again swats at his face…*)

WINSTON. Jeez, how do you stand all those feathers?

C. You can get used to anything over time – speaking of which, it's time for me to go, Winston.

(…*He stands…*)

WINSTON. Yeah, I know – line at the gate.

C. And a long one by now, no doubt.

(…*He extends a hand…*)

WINSTON. Thank you, C.

(…*She accepts it…*)

C. It's what I do.

WINSTON. No, I don't just mean for this… *(pointing to the stone)* …for everything… *(swatting feathers away)* …even the trail.

C. Hope it helps you find your way back.

WINSTON. Think it already has. Listen C, before you go, would you mind if I…um…can I ask you a question? A *personal* question?

C. Don't see why not.

WINSTON. Think you could tell me your *real* name?

C. Sure, but I'm warning you, it's…different.

WINSTON. Like Winston is normal?

C. OK, you asked for it…Clemencia.

WINSTON. Clemencia? Jeez that's…*pretty*…so what was all that *C for carver* jazz?

CLEMENCIA. Thought it sounded more official, less saint-like, and a lot better than Clem.

WINSTON. Heaven forbid you should stop being a wise-ass.

CLEMENCIA. Heaven forbid – now can I ask *you* a question? A *serious* question?

WINSTON. Guess I owe you one.

CLEMENCIA. Think you could give this whole miracle thing a second look?

WINSTON. Yeah…think I could do that.

CLEMENCIA. In that case I'll be leaving you two guys alone…pleasure meeting you, Winston.

WINSTON. Pleasure's mine, Clemencia. Hey, who knows, maybe we'll bump into each again one day.

CLEMENCIA. Never know, maybe one day we will.

WINSTON. Sure won't be hard to find you, I'll just look for the trail.

CLEMENCIA. You do that, Winston, you do that…goodbye.

*(…**WINSTON** watches as **CLEMENCIA** withdraws into the shadows. He turns to the grave, kneels before it, his eyes suddenly opening wide as he leaps to his feet and turns…)*

WINSTON. Wait! Clemencia, come back, I never paid you for…gone…no big deal, I'll just leave it with Miguel on the way out… *(reaching into his jacket)* …along with her…

(…He pulls out one bandana-less pocket, then the other…)

WINSTON. That's weird… *(looking around)* …must've fallen out and blown away.

(…He returns to the stone, dropping to one knee, as a panting burly **MAN** *in overalls enters, clanking tool belt in hand…)*

MAN. Yo, buddy!

(…a startled **WINSTON** *turns around…)*

WINSTON. Geez, you scared the hell out of…

MAN. …sorry, pal, traffic on the parkway was a bitch. Four car accident, bodies all over the road. Freakin' bloodbath, I tell ya', thought I'd never get here, but better late than never, right? Now where's the patient?

WINSTON. Patient? What patient?

(…Putting on a pair of thick glasses he removes from his overalls, the **MAN** *squints at a piece of paper he holds very closely…)*

MAN. Are you, uh, Winston McDonagh?

WINSTON. That's me.

MAN. Your Old Man's Francis Xavier McDonagh?

WINSTON. Francis *X.* McDonagh, that's right.

MAN. Then you got a grave that needs carvin'.

WINSTON. I did, but…

MAN. …well, I'm the guy who's carvin' it.

WINSTON. I'm confused.

MAN. You ordered a stone carver, I'm the stone carver, and I just drove all the way from Sunnyside to do it.

WINSTON. Wait a second, I think there's been some kind of misunder…

*(…Suddenly noticing a large, white feather slowly falling from above, **WINSTON** ponders its descent while scratching his head…)*

MAN. Hello?

*(…**WINSTON** watches the feather gently land atop the stone – he smiles…)*

MAN. Hey, pal, you OK?

WINSTON. How much do I owe you?

MAN. I didn't do anything yet.

WINSTON. There's been a slight…change of plans.

MAN. Change of…

*(…Seeing the freshly carved section of stone, the **MAN** bends and runs his hands over the work…)*

MAN. …mmm, not bad… *(straightens up)* …hey, wait a second, what's goin' on here? I came all the way from freakin' Queens to…

WINSTON. …will three hundred make us even?

MAN. Three hun… oh yeah.

*(…**WINSTON** takes out his wallet, pulls out three one hundred dollar bills, and hands them to the baffled **MAN**…)*

WINSTON. Sorry to make you come up here for nothing.

MAN. Any time, pal, *any* time… *(pocketing the cash)* …no one's gonna' believe *this*.

(…He vanishes in the shadows…)

WINSTON. You can say *that* again.

*(…**WINSTON** kneels before the stone…)*

WINSTON. Wish I could've been there for you, Dad…but don't worry, I'll be watchin' over everything from now on.

(…He runs his hand across the stone…)

You may not know this, but you've got some pretty fancy neighbors up here…just heard that The Babe's on the other side of that grotto. Think I'll take myself a little walk and pay my – *our* – respects. Besides, there are some statues over there I wanna' take a closer look at.

(…*He stands…*)

Love you, Dad…catch ya' on the way out.

(…**WINSTON** *walks past the stone, plucking the feather from it as he does…smiling, he examines the feather while walking off stage right, disappearing into the shadows, as lights dim into…*)

(*blackout*)

STAGE PROPERTIES

STAGE PROPS

- Headstone (front of which is angled from view, no markings evident)
- Three folding chairs
- Park bench
- Church pew

- Single, large feather attached to invisible wire or string

COSTUMES/PERSONAL PROPERTIES

WINSTON
- Zippered wind breaker, sweater, jeans, work shoes
- Wallet containing three bills and a business card
- Still-tagged Chicago Cubs baseball cap inside plastic shopping bag

MIGUEL THE GUIDE
- Black suit, tie & dress shoes – White shirt

C (CLEMENCIA)
- Well-worn puffy down vest, feathers clearly poking through
- White bandana – Denim shirt – Jeans – Muddy construction boots
- Utility belt with masonry tools, specifically mallet and chisel

TEENAGE WINSTON
- Blue suit, tie & brown dress shoes – Wrinkled white shirt

LOUISE
- Mourning clothes suitable for a conservative 60-year-old woman
- Handbag – Handkerchief

YOUNG WINSTON
- Little league uniform

THE OLD MAN
(Seen only from behind)
- Wind breaker – Baseball cap – Slacks – Sneakers

TOMMY
- Black suit, tie & dress shoes – White shirt

MAN
- Overalls – Work boots – Thick glasses – Wrinkled, folded work order
- Utility belt with masonry tools, specifically mallet and chisel

ABOUT THE AUTHOR

GEORGE CAMERON GRANT is an internationally produced author of eight full length plays, over twenty one acts, and numerous monologues. His latest one act play PUSH joins EPITAPH, a full-length play dedicated to his Father, and 4 X'MAS, his evening of one-act Christmas plays, as published members of the Samuel French family. He is an eight-time Samuel French Off Off Broadway Short Play Festival Finalist, most recently in 2009 for his play FORECLOSURE, which was also named a Finalist in the Nantucket Short Play Festival. PUSH was a Semi-Finalist in NYC's 2011 Strawberry Festival, garnering Best Actress and Best Director nominations. The Eastside Players of Madison (WI) High School entered PUSH into the 2012 Wisonsin High School Theatre Festival, receiving an All-State Award, and an Outstanding Actor Award for Scout Slava-Ross' portrayal of Eve. LEBEN, his full-length taking on pro-life/pro-choice issues, had its West Coast Premiere September 2012, at the Stage Door Repertory Theatre in Anaheim, CA. His new full-length Christmas play, HEAVEN CENT, written on commission for the same theater, had its World Premiere there on November, 2012, and was called "ONE OF THE YEAR'S 5 BEST" by Angela Hatcher of the Orange County News.

As Bookwriter/Lyricist/Composer, George recently completed a hugely successful series of staged readings of IN SEARCH OF ALICE, the second original musical he has created in collaboration with New York composer Michael J. Shapiro.

Also a two-time participant in the NY Independent Film Market, George has just completed his fourth screenplay DOUBLE EXPOSURE.

Composer of dozens of songs, George's PASS ON THE LOVE, performed by the legendary Persuasions, was featured in Spike Lee's DO IT A CAPPELLA.

George is an Addy Award winner for his graphic design work on August Wilson's FENCES, also creating for scores of motion pictures, including Academy Award® Winners and Nominees including ANVIL-THE STORY OF ANVIL, MONSTER, Y TU MAMA TAMBIEN, WHALE RIDER and AMADEUS.

George is the proud father of Elizabeth and Jenna. He is a member of BMI and the Dramatists Guild.

He can be reached on Facebook, Twitter: @cameron313, email: cameron313@aol.com or at www.georgecamerongrant.com.

OTHER GEORGE CAMERON GRANT TITLES AVAILABLE FROM SAMUEL FRENCH

PUSH
GEORGE CAMERON GRANT

Drama / 1m, 1f, 3boy(s), 3girl(s), 1m or f / Bare Stage
What would it take to push your child over the edge? Eve, a 16 year-old girl, has fallen asleep in the darkened, dingy corner of a deserted subway station, not far from the platform edge where Billy, her 18 year-old brother, chose to leave this world, and where she'll soon struggle to find the reasons NOT to follow him. ONE BULLIED CHILD IS ONE TOO MANY!